D1133160

Places in My Community

A Day at the Children's Museum

Celeste Bishop

illustrated by
Aurora Aguilera

PowerKiDS
press.

New York

Published in 2017 by The Rosen Publishing Group, Inc.
29 East 21st Street, New York, NY 10010

First Edition

Managing Editor: Nathalie Beullens-Maoui
Editor: Theresa Morlock
Book Design: Mickey Harmon
Illustrator: Aurora Aguilera

Cataloging-in-Publication Data

Names: Bishop, Celeste, author.
Title: A day at the children's museum / Celeste Bishop.
Description: New York : PowerKids Press, [2017] | Series: Places in my
   community | Includes index.
Identifiers: LCCN 2016027634| ISBN 9781499427738 (pbk. book) | ISBN
   9781508152873 (6 pack) | ISBN 9781499430165 (library bound book)
Subjects: LCSH: Children's museums–Juvenile literature. | Museums–Juvenile
   literature.
Classification: LCC AM8 .B57 2017 | DDC 069.083–dc23
LC record available at https://lccn.loc.gov/2016027634

Manufactured in the United States of America

CPSIA Compliance Information: Batch #BW17PK: For Further Information contact Rosen Publishing, New York, New York at 1-800-237-9932

Contents

Today is a special day. My family is going to the museum!

We're going to the children's museum.

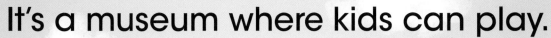

It's a museum where kids can play.

7

The children's museum is in
the middle of my city.

This area is called downtown.

The museum is in a big, tall building.

I can't wait to see what's inside!

Dad buys our tickets.

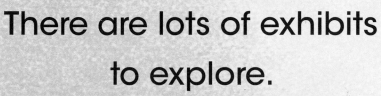

There are lots of exhibits
to explore.

I go to the bug exhibit first.

I learn about beetles and butterflies.

15

Next, I go to the rock exhibit.

16

I use a magnifying glass to see the rocks close-up.

One exhibit has a train.

My brother and I climb all over it.

I'm the conductor!

19

Our last stop is in the art room.

I paint a picture with my hands.
It's for my mom.

I like going to the children's museum. It's fun to play and learn!

22

Words to Know

butterfly

magnifying
glass

ticket

Index